How to Catch a Star

A Guide to Chasing Dreams

Stephen R. Vaughn

Jason Pavelchak

Illustrations by Scott Brinkley

How to Catch a Star

A Guide to Chasing Dreams

Printed by Lulu, Inc. For additional details visit lulu.com.

ISBN: 978-1-329-23442-0

Printed in the United States of America

First Edition

To the ones who back you and

the star that belongs to you.

Your dream awaits.

If you're going to do this right,
you have to do EVERYTHING
I tell you to do . . .

. . . no matter how weird it seems.

First, get a pen,

NOT a pencil.

The color doesn't matter.

Seriously, if you didn't get a pen, get one.

I'll tell you why in a second,

but GET A PEN.

You better have a pen, and here's why:

You need a pen because you're going to have to write things down. Don't panic, it's not that much.

But that's obvious. You probably really want to know why it matters if it's a pen or a pencil.

It HAS to be a pen because then you can't erase what you do. If you have a pencil you're going to use the eraser. That matters because if you're going to catch a star, you're going to make mistakes, and they're not the type of mistakes that you can just erase. Mistakes in life don't go away like that.

So, we're going to practice. You're going to write things with your pen that you wish you could erase, but you won't be able to.

Haha!

You need to learn that mistakes don't have to be bad. Mistakes always happen. You just have to figure out how to make them work out for the best, and you will. I'll help!

Now, flip to <u>the next page with words</u> and **RIP** it in half right down the middle . . .

t

h

i

s

w

a

y

YOU	CAN'T
YOU	CAN'T
YOU	CAN'T
YOU	CAN'T
YOU	CAN'T
YOU	CAN'T

CAN

WILL

CAN

WILL

CAN

WILL

You need to do these things

IN ORDER

with the paper you ripped out

(the one with the bad words):

1. Spit on it (make sure adults aren't watching).

2. Crumple it up.

3. Drop it on the floor.

4. Jump on it a couple of times.

5. Smash it with your foot like it's a bug (make sure bugs aren't watching).

6. Throw it away.

By now you might be wondering how any of this is going to help you catch a star.

That's why you're reading this, right?

You're right, we should talk about stars.

So, you need to put your pen to work.

Draw a star

below

in 10 seconds

or less . . .

10

9

8

7

6

5

4

3

2

1

0

I hope you're happy with your star.
I'm never happy with what I draw.

Now, before you go too far,
I feel like I need to tell you something.

I think you know, but it's okay if you don't.

If you don't know what I'm about to say,
don't hate me when I say it.

OK, you should turn the page.

Well . . .

Um . . .

You see . . .

The truth is . . .

We're not really going to catch a

((🖐)) star ((🖐))

See how I used the finger quotes there?

An actual "star" is . . .

"a massive, luminous sphere of plasma held together by its own gravity."

I even looked it up on Wikipedia
so you wouldn't think I was making it up.

The Sun is a "star,"
and it's bigger than a planet,
and its temperature is 10,000°F,
and that's just on the surface.

There's billions upon billions of "stars," and
most "stars" are even bigger and hotter.

So we're not going to catch a "star."

That would be bad!

When I say a star, I mean a dream.
A star is what you hope to achieve.

A star is what you want,
and I **don't** mean like a piece of pie
(mmm, now I'm hungry),
I mean like what you want your life to be.

A star is BIG and hard to catch.
That's why you need my help.

See, at first I didn't get it either . . .

The Wrong Kind of Dream

Now that you've gotten this far, I guess I should tell you who I am. My name is Max. I'm a boy (duh), and I probably like a lot of the same stuff you do. In fact, I'm probably a lot like you, which is why the first thing I tell you in my story shouldn't be a lie, not even a little one. I want you to trust me because I think I can really help you. So, I think I need to tell you something about me that's true, even if I can't say I'm all that proud of it:

I DON'T ~~ALWAYS~~ PAY ATTENTION. USUALLY

I don't recommend it, but come on, isn't that true for everyone?

27

Well, as it happens, I was having "an episode" at school one Friday not long ago. That's what I call it - "an episode" - when I zone out. I even use those finger quote things if someone asks me about it, but be careful with your parents. I've told that to them before, and then they go into this loooooooooooooooooooooooooooong speech and say something like, "Honey, you have to focus at all times, especially when you're in school, because blah blah blah blah blah blah ...."

I usually stop listening before the first sentence is over, but anyway, you know what I mean. It was one of those times when I'm in my seat at school staring at something but my mind is a million miles away. Plus, don't forget it was a Friday. That's practically the weekend! I have lots of "episodes" on Fridays.

Anyway, I was sitting in my seat during math, my brain floating away, when all of the sudden, my teacher, Mrs. Henderson, was standing next to me with her arms crossed, staring down at me with that teacher look. You know the one - it reaches into your lungs like icy fingers of doom and makes them stop working for a few seconds so you can't breathe.

"What are you doing, Max?" she asked me in a sweet voice.

If you're like me, you know that's the dangerous voice. That's when kids get lured in, thinking they're safe.

Instead of risking the wrong words, I shook my head and shrugged.

She smiled. "And what does that mean?"

I cleared my throat, trying to stall. Then I said the only thing I could think of, "I dunno."

Her smile stayed put. "What do you mean you don't know? You had to be doing something. What was it?"

I knew it was bad. Every kid in the class was looking at me at that point. It's like there was a wounded animal everyone could sense was about to get eaten. It's one of those things where nobody wants to watch because you know it's going to be ugly, but you still somehow can't take your eyes away.

Trying to think fast, I decided to start working on the problem I should have finished like five minutes ago. Sometimes that does the trick, and the teacher goes away satisfied that they got you working again, but NOT this time. Mrs. Henderson continued to loom over me, waiting for my answer. She wasn't going to let this one go.

"Well?" she said again, not quite as sweetly as before

I had to come up with something. "I was . . . thinking."

"Thinking about what?"

What was I supposed to say? I didn't know
what I was thinking about! My brain was somewhere
else. It was captured in some fog in space or
something or somewhere while the aliens and
dinosaurs wrestled Spongebob for the next unicorn
ride.

"I don't know," I finally said.

"You don't know?" Then her eyes narrowed.
The smile was gone. "Max, you mean to tell me
you've been sitting there for ten minutes, staring at

the cat poster on the wall, and you can't even tell me one thing you were thinking about? **One** thing?" she repeated.

I looked at the cat poster. There was a little white kitten with a pencil in its hand (or paw I guess, or whatever) writing a note. I don't even like cats.

Some of the students were laughing, quietly so they didn't get in trouble along with me. Others were trying to hold it in but failing, with their cheeks puffed out all red from trying to keep the smiles off their faces.

I tried desperately to think of one thought that had gone through my head, but I honestly could not think of a single thing. "No, ma'm." That's when I realized I should have just made something up. I could have said anything - cake, sharks, the beach, why big toes are so big. But no, I had to say **nothing**!

Mrs. Henderson opened her mouth, ready to let the cannons rain down on me, but nothing came out. It's like she was stuck. She knew she was supposed to be mad, but I think she just felt sorry

for me. She looked at me
and her face was sort of
like when you see a
three-legged dog
running. It was . . .
sad. She walked away,
not even saying another
word. She just shook her
head.

I looked at the other kids, and suddenly I felt
lost. Why didn't I know what I was thinking about?
I knew what the others kids were thinking about.
Alexis was thinking about soccer, that's all she ever
did or talked about or thought about. Darren always
read books. Kelly couldn't stop drawing. Hugo played
Minecraft. Gavin knew everything about the
football team. Jannel sang every song you'd ever
heard of. I could name something for just about
every kid in the class, except me.

Why did I know what everyone else was
thinking about, but not me? It didn't make sense. It

was so bad that I didn't even get homework over the weekend. That might sound good, but this was one of those things where you know you deserve the punishment.

And I didn't get it.

I wasn't even worth the trouble.

I had to figure this out. I couldn't be the kid who drooled on himself during class staring at a cat poster without even knowing what he was thinking about.

MISSION: WHAT DO I THINK ABOUT???

Danger at Dinner

I'm sure you agree that it was better for my parents not to know anything about my "episode," so when I got home from school I went straight to my room. I figured it would be best to avoid them as much as possible because if your parents are like mine, they seem to have a way of finding things out even if you have no intention whatsoever of telling them. I don't know if it's like a parent super-power or what. So the way I saw it, if they didn't see me they couldn't find anything out.

After throwing my backpack on the floor I sat down at my desk. I had to clear away a half-eaten snack from the day before and a bunch of papers.

It's funny, I never had a clue where they came from, but there were **always** papers. It was the same with my desk at school. Anytime I wanted to find something, it took forever because it was somehow in the middle of a hundred other papers that had crawled out of some paper-monster's belly.

When I could finally see some of the actual desk (oh, so that's what it looks like!), I took out a notebook and a half-sharpened pencil. It was time to get to work. I had to figure out what to think about.

I spent over an hour hard at work, and by dinnertime my paper was completely filled.

Unfortunately, when I looked down at my handiwork all I could do was frown. I'd drawn an evil blob devouring a city, a stick figure with a curly mustache, several scribbles I couldn't really remember even doing, a giant number 4, and at least fifty dots. Not my best work . . . but not my worst!

I do have to say that I'm pretty proud of my curly mustache.

So anyway, after my failed attempt I didn't eat much of my dinner because I was so **LOST** in thought, and then it happened again.

"Honey, you've barely touched your food. What are you thinking about?" my mom asked.

I couldn't believe she'd asked me that. I was furious! I slammed my fist on the table and shouted, "Ahhhh!" It came out more like a choking whale sound than an angry kid sound, but at least it was loud. "I don't know what I'm thinking about!"

My mom and dad looked at each other with some sort of unspoken secret parent communication while my little sister stuck her tongue out at me.

"You know not to yell at your mother like that," my dad finally said. "All she did was ask you what you're thinking about."

I wrinkled my nose and gave him the meanest look I could. I even clenched my teeth and shook my head really fast to get my point across. "I know, but I don't **know** what I'm thinking about!" I stomped my feet in frustration.

"Whoa, Max. Calm down. You're not in trouble or anything. We're not trying to be nosy. It's just plain to see that you're upset. We want to help."

I slumped down in my chair and glared at the ceiling.

My mom sighed and said in her quiet voice, "It helps to talk about things. Were you thinking about something that upset you? Did something happen at school today?"

How do they always know?

Parents and their superpowers!

Well I wasn't going to fall for this one. It was just a lucky guess. I made a gargling sound, but it sounded pretty weird without any water in my mouth, like a grizzly bear gagging.

"Come on. You can trust us,"
my dad said. He even made my little
sister leave the room, which I have to say did help.

"It's just . . . well . . . I don't know what to
think about."

It sounded silly even saying it out loud.

My mom squinted, and I could tell she was
confused. I knew I had to explain more. "Mom, all
the other kids know what to think about, but I
don't have a clue."

"But, haven't you been thinking of stuff this
whole time we were eating dinner?"

I shrugged. "Yeah, but I don't know what. I
was trying to think of what to think about."

My dad laughed, which I wasn't very happy
about, but then he said something that really made
me think, "What do you **want** to think about?"

It's so important that I **bolded** it and underlined it.

What did I **want** to think about?

"I don't know," I said. "What do you think about?"

"Hmm," he said, thinking it over, "I think about things that I like, things I care about. You must have things that you like. Aren't you passionate about anything?"

I didn't like the sound of the word passionate. It made me think of guy-girl romance stuff. NO THANK YOU.

"I don't want to think about girls, DAD." I said the dad part as sarcastically as I could.

"That's not what I'm talking about."

"Then what does passionate mean?"

"It means that you really care strongly about something, more than most things. If you're passionate about something, you want to do that more than practically anything else, and you'll give other things up for it."

"So you're not secretly talking about girls or

41

something?" I had to double-check.

"No, Max. You can be passionate about anything," he said.

I had a lot more to think about. "Mom, I'm sorry I yelled at you. Thanks for making me talk. You too, Dad. May I be excused to go up to my room. I need to think."

My Star

The first thing I did when I got to my room was rip out the page in my notebook with all the doodles. Then, on my next page I wrote "Things I Like:"

I had a couple of things to write down right away, but then it was tough to think of many more. Still, I kept thinking. I thought all night and added some things here and there. I knew some of them probably didn't fit, but I put them down anyway. I didn't want to miss anything.

Before I go on, you need to try. Get your pen and write down things you like:

It was weird. On a Friday night I'd usually be watching a movie or playing video games or picking on my sister or something like that, but this was important. It's not every day your teacher feels so sorry for you that she doesn't give you a punishment you deserve because you're that pathetic.

It got dark outside, and I watched the stars pop up outside my window. Eventually I pretty much gave up on adding things to my list and turned out the lights. I didn't go to sleep, though. I sat there at my desk, staring at the stars and thinking about my list. I could see the stars so much easier with the lights out. And without so many distractions to look at, it was a lot easier to focus on the things I'd written down.

Maybe I was delirious from staying up late, but I kept finding that there was one star I always came back to, and one thing on my list. I can't say it was a special star or anything. It wasn't bigger or brighter or twinkling or any of that. It was just there, among the thousands of other stars. Still, I

44

always caught myself looking at that same star and thinking about that same thing from my list, and that's when it hit me:

THAT'S MY STAR.

I fell asleep thinking about my star and that maybe there's a star for everyone if they look, just like everybody has something to think about if they think about it.

That night I slept the best I can ever remember sleeping, but I woke up early the next morning, way earlier than I usually do on a weekend. It wasn't that bad sort of waking up either, like when your eyes refuse to open because there is no way you want to get out from under your warm, snuggly sheets. Nope, I woke up and my brain was already churning things out. And guess what . . . I knew exactly what I was thinking about.

 I stayed in my room most of the rest of the weekend. It became my workshop. Every now and then I went to the garage and borrowed one of my dad's tools from his toolbox or dug around in the big closet by the kitchen to find what I needed. There was some pounding and banging and sawing and hammering and even an accident or two, but little

holes in the wall can easily be covered with a poster. My sister fussed a lot, my mom fussed a little, but my dad never did. He was more curious than anything, but NOBODY was allowed in my room.

Finally, when Monday morning came and it was time to go to school, I was done.

I had it.

I knew what I thought about.

My passion.

My dream.

My star.

Too bad I didn't know that my story was only getting started. It turns out that it's not that easy to catch a star.

I know you can't wait to read about what happened when I went to school, but first I've got a really important **MISSION** for you, so you better still have that pen. I'm giving you plenty of space below. What I want you to do is make a list of what **tools** you **think** you need to catch a star. You can even draw pictures if you want . . .

Revealed

Imagine how I felt walking into class Monday morning. Talk about swag! It was like I had an Olympic gold medal hanging around my neck, and if you ask me, it was just as good. See, it actually **was** hanging around my neck! I'd worked all weekend building a box to put my star in, and it was

AMAZING!

As soon as I walked in the door everyone noticed, and there was a mad rush like I was a celebrity or something. Everybody wanted to touch my box, and I had to explain like a million times what it was. Finally Mrs. Henderson walked over and chased everyone back to their seats.

"What's going on, Max?" she asked.

I held the box out in the palm of my hands
and grinned. "Look! I caught a star!"

She had a doubtful look.

"I mean, it's not like a real star up in the sky.
I know that. But I saw my star this weekend and
built this box to put it in. Now I'll always have it
and know what to think about." I grinned. "I know
what I think about!"

"Just don't let it get you in trouble," she said
as she walked away, but I also noticed she had a
little smile when she said it.

"I won't," I promised.

That day I didn't hear a single thing that happened in class. All I could think of was my star. It was incredible to know what I thought about, and to think about it! It's all I could do.

At lunch, everyone wanted to sit with me. At recess, practically every kid swarmed around me to see the box again. All day long I showed my box off and told anyone who would listen about my star.

When I went home I was exhausted. It's tough work being a superSTAR. Ha! See what I did there, with the STAR thing?

Answer this question . . .

What did I do wrong in school?

Don't worry, it's NOT graded or anything like that. I don't care if you write in complete sentences or spell words right or use punctuation.

I'll even tell you that my answer is only 6 words long, so you don't have to write much.

Just make sure you use your pen!

Write your answer down and THEN you can check my answer on the next page.

What did I do wrong in school?

Answer - I didn't pay attention in class.

Remember my teacher telling me
not to let my star get me in trouble?

OOPS.
Not a very good start.

Sure, she didn't catch me,
but things have a way of catching up to you.

Copy Cat

The next day I was in for quite a surprise at school. I was a few minutes later than usual (I was busy thinking about my star and forgot to brush my teeth but my mom wouldn't let me leave until I had minty-fresh breath so I had to go back upstairs and scrub-a-dub-dub my teeth). So I was later than usual, and when I walked into the classroom nobody came to look at my box like before. Instead, they were all huddled around another kid. I didn't know what was up at first, but then I saw it . . .

But before I tell you what I saw, I want to make sure you know how I was feeling. Do you know that game where you copy everything the other person says? I'm sure you do, and it's not even really a game I guess. You pretty much just do it to annoy someone, which isn't that nice when you think about it like that. Anyway, you know how annoying it can be if someone does it to you. They literally just say everything you say. Some kids even copy everyTHING you do, like smiling and blinking and turning their head and crossing their arms and EVERYTHING. Ahhhhhhhhhhhh!!!!!! Just thinking about it makes me want to scream.

And I'm not talking about the slightly annoyed feeling you have after like a minute. I mean that feeling when whoever is copying you refuses to stop, even though you've asked them politely, nicely, rudely, meanly, and every other -ly word you can think of. Imagine that feeling when you're ready to blow like a volcano and multiply it times googolplex.

That's how I felt.

And what could make me feel that way?

This other kid the class was huddled around, well . . .

He had my box.

My box.

He had MY box.

MY BOX!

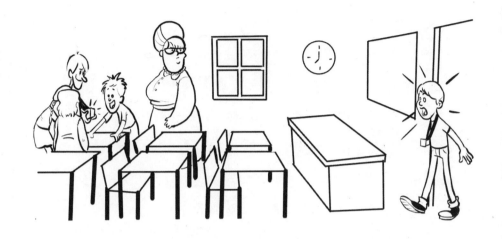

MY
BOX!!!!!!

Honestly, it wasn't my box. My box was still hanging around my neck, which of course it had to be. I ONLY took it off when I slept, and then I always kept it on the desk right beside my bed where I'd first seen my star.

I ALWAYS had my box with me.

But this kid had my box. I went over and stared at it, glared it, studied it, inspected it, examined it. Everything was the same.

It was the same size and shape. It was the same color as mine. It had the same markings and even the same scratch I'd accidentally made on the bottom with one of my dad's tools.

It was my box. The only difference was that it wasn't my box.

I was about to do something really not smart when Mrs. Henderson came over and made us all sit down because it was time for class to start, but then she said something that really threw me for a loop.

"Hey, nice box! Did you get a star, too?" she asked the other kid.

"Yep!" he said with the biggest smirk I've ever seen.

"I guess that's the new thing," she muttered. "Must be the latest trend or something."

I was fuming. I thought my head would surely pop off

or the seat would melt

or the entire room would just EXPLODE!

But it didn't.

And I didn't hear a thing that happened in class, again.

All I could think about was MY STAR around HIS neck.

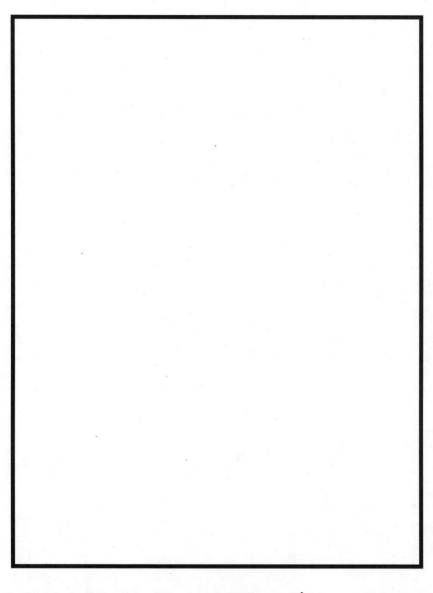

I just told you the **maddest** I've ever been.

What's the maddest you've ever been?

I don't know about you, but I like pictures.

Big Bad Bully

I'm sure you know I couldn't NOT do something. I had to. I stewed all morning about that box, and I was boiling over by the time I could do something about it at lunch.

As soon as I got into the cafeteria I forced my way into the seat beside him and didn't even say hi.

Still, I tried to be calm about it, I really did. I figured if I just talked to the star-stealer he would apologize and get rid of his box when he saw how upset I was.

"What's the idea? Why'd you copy my box?"

Okay, maybe I didn't use the nicest voice, but I didn't yell or anything.

"I liked it," he said. "And I wanted one, so I made one for myself."

I didn't know what to say for a second. It was sort of a compliment, saying he liked my box, but then he said something that pushed me over the edge . . .

"It was pretty easy to make."

He even grinned when he said it, like he KNEW it would make me mad.

Maybe you've had this happen to you, where you're not even in control of what you're doing. Well, I was so angry my body was shaking. I don't even remember thinking about what I was doing, but it was like some evil monster came alive inside me. I saw a couple of kids nearby lean away as I grabbed my bologna and mustard sandwich (which I never understand my parents giving me since I don't like it).

I peeled the top piece of bread off and in a flash slammed the rest of the sandwich into the star-stealer's face. I twisted my hand back and forth like I was scrubbing a window. I rubbed that slimy meat all over his mouth and cheeks as the mustard squirted up into his nose.

He was so shocked he fell backwards off his seat and plopped onto the ground. As he gasped for breath and wiped the meat-juice and mustard from his face, I snatched the box from around his neck and threw it on the ground. I stood up and stomped on it as hard as I could.

CRACK! It sounded like a branch breaking in half as pieces of his box flew in every direction.

That's when I came to my senses and a flood of realizations came over me. My classmates were looking at me like I was a madman. The kid on the cafeteria floor was almost in tears. Bits of my sandwich and his box were all over the place. And several teachers were rushing over. Everything was a blur, and before I could blink, I was in the principal's office getting picked up by my mom.

Did you see the title of my last chapter?
I bet you didn't think I was going to be the
"Big Bad Bully."

It's not a good thing to be the bad guy.

*Advice - don't do that.

Excuses

I wish I was smarter, and I hope you're smarter than I was. See, even after my teacher fussed at me, and the principal scolded me, and my parents yelled at me, and I cried (don't laugh, you'd cry too), and I wrote an apology note, and I even called and apologized, I still didn't get it.

I was convinced it wasn't **MY** fault. It was the star-stealer's fault. He shouldn't have copied my box, and he shouldn't have said what he said. If he hadn't done that, I never would have shoved lunch meat in his face. I was getting in trouble when **HE** was the one who started it all.

I thought about it every second for the rest of the week.

At school, the other kids were staying away from me in case I lost my temper again, which wasn't fair. AND I couldn't wear my box anymore, which wasn't fair either.

I still kept it in my pocket. I mean, I **HAD** to keep it with me. It was my star, but nobody wanted to see it anymore.

So everybody at school avoided me, my parents were upset with me, and I couldn't even take my star out. Things were pretty bad. The only good thing was that I still had my star. That's something nobody was going to take away from me. I knew what to think about.

But then things got worse, a lot worse.

I bet things are the same for you at your

school, but on Fridays I always have like eighteen tests. I think it's a conspiracy with teachers to try to make one of the best days of the week less fun. Fun and Friday go together, not tests and Friday.

That Friday was no different, but how was I supposed to know that it was a **BIG** test day? By **BIG** test day I mean that I had like five tests that covered weeks of material we'd been going over in class.

Did I have a clue?

Nope.

Had I studied?

Nope.

Was I ready?

Nope.

Did I do well?

Nope.

I didn't need to see my grades to know I'd bombed every single one of them.

It was so unfair!

If it hadn't been for that star-stealer I knew I would have been fine. Instead, I'd had to spend time writing apology notes and worrying about everybody else thinking I was a lunatic who shoved bologna in people's faces. How was I supposed to focus with all of that going on? Besides, I had my star to think about. You can't tell me that a test is more important than a star!

I decided not to tell my parents about the **BIG** test day. I'd wait until I got my official grades back. Maybe I'd get lucky and pass some of them, or maybe Mrs. Henderson would spill coffee on the papers, or even lose them. I could hope!

But when Monday came around and we got our grades back, I found out that I wasn't so lucky. I barely even got half the questions right on any of the tests, which was worse than I'd thought. And I knew what was coming . . .

. . . parent-teacher conference.

Decisions

I'm sure you can guess how things went - not good. I had no idea what was coming, though. I never would have thought my parents could do what they were about to.

After the parent-teacher conference, which I didn't have to be part of (phew), my parents came home and had me come into the dining room to talk. The three of us sat around the table, and they just looked at me for a few minutes. It was a little eerie. They didn't say anything, they just looked at me.

I could tell they were sad. I'd never failed tests before, not like this. Maybe a quiz here or there, but never a test. I've always gotten  pretty decent grades. I'd also never gone to the principal's office before or gotten into a "fight" (which is what they called me shoving my sandwich into that kid's face).

All that had changed in a matter of days, though. Now I was the bad guy, the bully, the crazy one. Unfair was all I could think about, but I kept my mouth shut.

Finally my dad spoke. He didn't seem mad. He simply said, "Take your box out and put it on the table."

I was shocked for a second. "What does my star have to do with any of this?"

"Do what your dad asked," my mom said.

I had a bad feeling, but if I've learned anything since I was a baby, it's to do what your parents ask. It's only worse if you fight with them, so I dug into my pocket and set it on the table. I scowled so they'd know I wasn't happy.

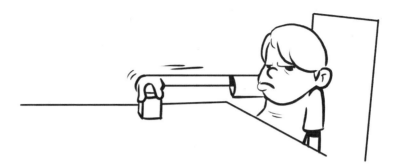

I could hear my sister stomping around in her room. Why did she get to play around while this was going on? So unfair. She did stuff all the time and always got away with it.

My dad moved my star to the middle of the table and out of my reach, which I really didn't like.

"I've got an important question for you," he said. "I want you to think before you say anything, and I want you to be honest."

I shrugged.

"Would you have gotten in a fight if it wasn't for this box?"

"Yeah," I blurted out without thinking. "It was that kid's fault for stealing my idea. He started it. If he hadn't done that then there wouldn't have been a 'fight' at all." I even used air quotes with my fingers around the word "fight" to make sure they knew I didn't think it was fair to call it a "fight."

My mom cleared her throat. "Your father asked you to think first."

I crossed my arms and rolled my eyes. "That kid started it, not my star."

My dad waited for a minute, like that was going to change my mind. Then he asked, "Okay, since you don't seem to get what's going on here, let me ask it another way. If you had never made this box, would you have gotten in a fight."

"No. Obviously. If I didn't have my star then there wouldn't have been anything to copy."

"And would you have failed those tests if you'd never made this box?"

I really didn't like where this was going. "You can't take my star! It's mine."

"Answer the question," my mom said. "Would you have failed your tests?"

"Probably not," I mumbled. My mom gave me a look. "Fine. No I wouldn't have failed the tests.

Most likely," I added quietly. "But it's not fair to take my star. It's mine. It's what I think about. It's not a bad thing!"

"It's not a bad thing," my dad agreed, which made me feel a lot better. "In fact, it's a great thing."

"So you're not going to take it?"

"Can we?" my mom said in a tone I couldn't quite figure out.

"No!" I said as fast as I could.

My dad looked at me with one of those serious adult looks. "Then we have something important we need to talk about."

I squirmed in my seat, confused about what was going on. If they weren't going to take my star, what was this whole thing about?

"What exactly is in that box?" my mom asked.

"My star. It's what I think about. You know that."

"That's great, but is that it?"

I looked at my dad for support, but all he did was nod. What did a nod even mean at this point? I had no idea. "I don't know what you mean. You just said it's a great thing."

My dad spoke up, "It's great that you have your star, but do you really?"

I was starting to get frustrated. "I don't know what you're talking about," I said louder than I probably should have.

"Have you actually caught your star?"

I thought about it and finally had to shake my head.

"That's what we mean," my dad said. "You say that your star is what you think about, so what do you think about?"

"You just said it yourself. I think about my star."

"And is that all you want? Do you just want to think about your star? Or do you want to catch your star?"

I snorted. "I want to catch my star." I wanted to add a sarcastic duh, but I knew that was a really bad idea.

"So how are you going to do it?"

I'd never thought about that. All I'd ever thought about since getting my star was . . . well . . . my star.

"I don't know," I answered.

"Then you have a decision to make. You can think about your star or you can catch your star. See, you can think about your star all you want, but if all you ever do is think about it, you're never going to catch it. You have to do something about it. You have to act, and your thoughts should give purpose to your actions. If your thoughts and your actions aren't working together, then you're not going to get anywhere, especially not anywhere you want to go."

My mom sighed. "Think about your actions lately. Is all that thinking about your star giving any sort of worthy purpose to your actions?"

"No," I said bitterly.

"You might not think that a math test or a writing test or how you treat someone has anything to do with your star, but it does. How can you ever hope to catch your star if you can't pass your tests at school? How will you ever reach your star if everyone around you is in your way and you're fighting against them?"

"I've never thought about it like that."

"Well it's time that you do. It's great that you've got your star to think about, but you better figure out what you're going to do about it."

My dad looked at my mom with a suspicious expression and then turned back to me. "There's one other option."

"What's that?" I asked.

"You can let your star go. You can give it up."

Okay, whatever you do, don't make the mistake I did.

And I'm not even talking about the shoving meat and mustard in someone's face or failing all my tests (of course don't do that).

Instead, don't think that thinking is enough.

The real mistake I made was that I thought I had my star when I actually hadn't even started chasing it.

Knowing where your star is isn't enough.

FINALLY I realized that, but was it too late? I'd messed up pretty badly, and I still hadn't really figured out what to do. I had to decide.

Grit

That's a funny name for a chapter, isn't it? I hope you don't know what it means because you'll figure it out in this chapter. If you already know what it means you can pat yourself on the back because I sure didn't know what it meant for a while. If you look it up that's kind of like cheating, but I don't mind. That's not what this is about. I'd rather you know than not! You'll have to know eventually if you want to catch your star.

Anyway, at school all the next week I didn't take my star out of my pocket during class. I had it with me, but I didn't think about it. I paid attention in class like I was supposed to and tried to have the right actions. I said hi to people and held the door and picked up my trash and did all my work.

The only time I took my star out was at recess. I sat on a bench and took it out of my pocket and held it. I honestly didn't even think about it all that much. I just held it.

If you want to know the truth, I was sad. Why was it that something so good was turning out to be such a bad thing?

By Friday I was back to myself. I took tests all morning like we always did on Fridays, but this time I knew I'd done good. My parents would be happy. I was even getting along with everyone, even if they still kept their distance.

I sat on the same bench at recess and took out my star, and I held it like I had all week. And I was sadder than ever.

You know why? I realized that my star was nothing but trouble. When I'd let myself think about my star, I'd gotten in a fight and failed everything at school. This week I'd ignored my star and done great with everything. If that was how it was, I knew what I had to do.

I spotted a trashcan across the playground and then gazed at the box one last time. I thought about the beautiful star and the night I'd found it. I tried not to cry. The last thing you want to do is cry at school. Still, there was a huge lump in my throat that I just couldn't swallow.

Finally I closed my eyes and stood up. I had to do it. I had to get rid of my star. Wasn't it the right thing to do? If all it did was get me in trouble, I had to let it go.

Did I mention I was sad? It didn't feel right in my heart, but it seemed right in my head, so I stood over the trashcan, ready to throw it away.

"Hey, man, I want to show you something."

Just as I was about to let my box drop into the muck of a school garbage can (and they're the worst, trust me) someone came up behind me and dragged me back to the bench.

This was the first time someone from my class had taken time to do anything with me since the fight, so I was pretty surprised.

"Sure," I said. "What is it?"

"Don't get mad," he said. Then he acted like he was rethinking this whole thing, and I thought he might run off as unexpectedly as he'd come.

"I won't," I promised.

He glanced around nervously and then took something out of his pocket. He slowly opened his hand and smiled.

"It's my star," he said.

It was a box like mine, but it really wasn't the same at all. The color and the markings and even the shape were different. It wasn't very pretty, but I wasn't going to tell him that, and boys don't say things are pretty anyway, so forget I even mentioned that word.

"That's great," I said.

"You're not mad?" he double-checked.

"No," I said, and I really wasn't. He hadn't copied me at all. This was obviously HIS star.

Then I remembered what I was about to do and knew I had to warn him.

"But I have to tell you, my star's been nothing but trouble. I'm about to get rid of it."

The boy shook his head. "You can't do that! You inspired me to get mine!"

I shrugged. "That's great, but like I said, all my star does is get me in trouble. I really really hope yours doesn't, but I have to get rid of mine. I do better without it."

"Max, your star isn't getting you in trouble. YOU are getting you in trouble. Besides, if it's your star, won't it always be there? You can't just get rid of a star. Even if you throw it away, won't it still be there?"

I shrugged again. "I don't know. When I smashed that box in the cafeteria, everything inside got smashed right along with it."

The boy laughed. "There wasn't any star in that box. Don't you know anything? He had the same box, but that's it. Think about it, how could two people have the same star? We've all got our own! He copied your box, but he can't steal your star. Besides, did you see anything in that box when you stomped on it?"

"I don't think so."

"Exactly. I don't know about yours, but my box is full of stuff, man. It would turn that cafeteria into a zoo if you let my star out of its box."

My box did have stuff in it. I didn't really know what, but there was definitely something. Maybe he was right. Maybe I couldn't let go of my star.

"You're right," I finally said.

"Of course I am!"

"Why would I ever give up on my star? I can't let go of it."

"Now you're talking!"

I smirked. "And nothing can make me!" I studied the box in my hand. "But, what do we do?"

His eyes got big and he smiled so wide I could see every one of his teeth. "We catch 'em!"

I smiled back. "Thanks, Carlos."

At that moment I didn't have a clue how, but I knew I was going to catch my star.

No matter what.

I had decided.

I was determined.

Resolute.

Full of **GRIT**.

So now do you think you know what
"GRIT" is?

If not, that's okay.
Just check out the **bottom** of the page.
Remember, I WANT you to have the right
answer.

Have you ever faced a situation
where you needed grit?
What was it?

Change

It helped having someone on my team, someone to encourage me. We talked about our stars everyday at recess, specifically how to catch them. We realized that our stars were very different, but we also realized that catching stars (any stars) have a lot in common no matter how different they are. Catching stars is a big thing, and to catch our stars we were going to have to start with some basic skills. As it turns out, school was a great place to develop those skills.

At school, I had opportunities every day to work hard, to figure out problems, to plan and organize, to interact with others respectfully, and overall just how to get things done the right way.

I wasn't writing stories to complete a class assignment anymore, I was working to become a better writer because I saw that being a better writer would help me catch my star.

In math, I figured out that learning how to

work through a problem would be a HUGE part of catching my star. I didn't have to be the best in the world or anything, but I couldn't stink at addition or subtraction or multiplication or division if I was trying to catch a star! And I couldn't make a mess of half the word problems like I always had. I had to take my time and make sure I was doing it ALL right.

It was the same with reading. I knew I'd have to read like a MILLION things about my star to understand it better so I could catch it. I could become a better reader at school! Even if I wasn't reading about my star, I could still develop my skills.

Science, social studies, music, art, PE, computer stuff - all of it would help me catch my star. It's weird, but I wasn't satisfied any longer with decent grades. I wanted the best grades. I wanted to be **EXCELLENT** at everything. If I couldn't master these skills it would be that much harder to catch my star.

Being good at stuff wasn't even an option

anymore. I HAD to learn to be good at things to catch my star. I knew it would take a while for me to get good at certain things (we all have our weaknesses, right?!), but if I kept working hard, I knew I could do it.

It wasn't just the academic stuff either, there were all kinds of opportunities at school. How would I catch a star if I couldn't keep my desk organized? How would I catch a star if I couldn't find my homework? How would I catch a star if I didn't listen to what my teacher said? If I forgot my jacket outside at recess, how would I remember all the stuff I'd need to so I could catch my star?

It's like my eyes were opened. I was seeing things differently than I'd ever seen them before. Now that I recognized all those things would help me catch my star, I **WANTED** to do them. It sounds crazy, but each time I worked hard in class or proved myself on a test it was like taking a step toward my star. I couldn't exactly prove it, but somehow I knew I was getting closer. It's like I had finally begun on the journey to catching my star.

I guess that's how I was supposed to do it, by doing the right things, and now that I knew I was on the right track, I wanted to take more and more steps everyday to get closer and closer. Other than the regular class stuff, I cleaned up after myself, and even others sometimes. I tried to be nice to people. I was respectful to my teachers. I tried to help whenever I could. I was less careless, more purposeful, less sloppy, more neat, less stressed, more patient.

Perfect? Not even close! I still yelled at my sister too much (but less) and my room was mostly a wreck (but not completely) and there were still papers everywhere in my desk (but not quite as many).

It was what my parents had been trying to tell me all along - my star should give my actions a purpose. I saw that purpose now, and my actions were different than they'd ever been.

But

Yep, I named this chapter but, but it's not butt. I left off the second t. There's something else about catching a star that I learned very quickly - it's not easy. Last chapter you might think it seemed a little easy to make all those changes, **BUT** I hadn't faced any real challenges yet, and there are always challenges, obstacles, things to overcome. That's when and where grit comes into play.

So, things were going great, for a while. Then, my teacher stood up at the end of a gloomy Wednesday afternoon and announced the biggest project of the year.

A group project.

You know who was in my group, right?

Not Carlos.

Nope.

The star-stealer.

That's another thing teachers always seem to do. I mean, how do you always get stuck in a group with the last person on earth you'd want to be with?

Oh, and not to mention my other two group members were girls.

And it got worse. The project was so big we'd also have to do some work outside of school. Together. Outside of school. Together.

I moaned as the bell rang and it was time to go home.

The star-stealer found me in the hall and stood next to me. I know I'd apologized and all that, but let's just say we still weren't exactly friends, which wasn't a surprise. It would be hard to forgive somebody who rubbed bologna and mustard in your face in front of everybody in the cafeteria.

"This will be fun," he said to me.

"Yep."

"I already talked to the girls. We're meeting at my house this Saturday after lunch. You're supposed to bring the markers."

I nodded.

"You know the address?"

"Yep."

"Good. I'm looking forward to it." He slapped me HARD on the back and walked off snickering.

I did not have a good feeling about this.

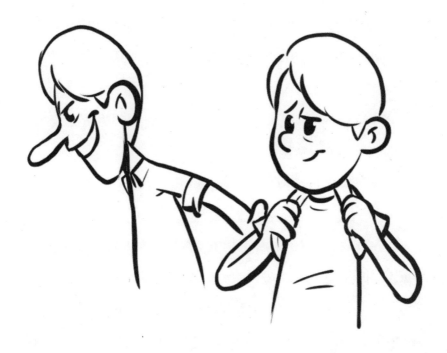

Uh-Oh

Saturday afternoon came in a flash. I made sure to get there on time with the markers, just like I'd been told. My heart beat faster than usual as I rang the doorbell. Then the door opened and the star-stealer waved to my mom as he pulled me inside. I watched my mom drive off, and the door slammed shut.

"We're upstairs," he said. "We've been waiting."

"This is when you told me to get here," I said confused.

I walked into the room and the girls were already sitting on the floor with papers spread out in front of them. I said hi and they gave me those fake smiles we all use sometimes. I could tell they weren't happy with me.

I sat down across from them and took the box of markers out of my backpack.

"What's that?" Jenna asked.

"Markers. That's what I was supposed to bring."

The girls rolled their eyes and whispered something to each other I couldn't quite hear. Then Brianna took out a deluxe super-collection of every marker color that's ever been created. I'm not even kidding when I say the box was practically the size of my bed at home.

Suddenly the box of markers in my hand felt like stinky trash. I stuck it back in my bag and shrugged.

"Sorry," I mumbled.

"Well, at least you brought the poster board, right?"

I sighed. "No. I thought I was supposed to bring markers."

Brianna threw her hands up. "Great," she said

sarcastically. "How are we supposed to do **ANYTHING** then?"

The star-stealer laughed from his bed. "Hey, no big deal. We've got everything planned out. You heard the teacher. There always tends to be someone in the group who doesn't pull their own weight. We can do this."

He was talking like I wasn't even there, and he was talking like I'd done something wrong.

"Hey!" I growled at him. "You told me to bring markers, so if I brought the wrong thing it's your fault. And if I'm late, it's your fault for telling me the wrong time."

The girls scooted back.

"You're scaring the girls," the star-stealer said. "You're not going to snap again, are you?" He looked at the girls. "Don't worry, I'll get my parents in here. We knew this might happen."

I was flabbergasted. "What are you talking about?"

One of the girls squeaked, and then Jenna said, "It's fine. We can do the project. Just calm down. It's okay if you messed up."

"I didn't mess up!"

Why was I still the crazy kid? I'd changed. I worked hard now and did the right thing and even treated people mostly good. This was so unfair!

"Remember," the star-stealer said, "we get to give each other a grade, so it's no big deal. We'll know who did all the work."

The monster inside me wanted to get out again and throw every single marker at the star-stealer as hard as I could. He'd planned this whole thing out. He'd set me up to fail. All my hard work seemed useless right now, and I'd have given anything for another bologna and mustard sandwich.

I knew just what to do with it.

I was mad, angry, irate, livid! I put my hands over my face, trying not to explode. I had to think instead. I had to.

I took a deep breath. I felt my star in my pocket and knew I had to be stronger than this. I had to overcome. I needed GRIT. I couldn't give in to the monster inside me and go backward. This could be another step on the way to catching my star, a BIG step, and I couldn't give up. I couldn't let this beat me. I had to be greater than my problem, just like in math or science or any obstacle in life.

"I'm sorry," I finally said. "I didn't mean to mess up. What do we need to do? I can do the poster tomorrow. I'll have my mom take me to the store tonight."

The girls looked at each other and scooted closer, ready to move on. They pointed at the papers and were just ready to explain what they'd been working on when the star-stealer butted in.

"Whoa! I don't want him doing the poster.

That's the most important part of the project. I don't trust him to do it right."

The girls frowned. "But the teacher said to let everyone do part of the project. That's the part we need done."

"I'll do it," I said. "I want to do it, and I'll do a good job. I promise."

The girls were more than happy to let me work on it. They organized the papers to hand to me.

Brianna said, "Get the information on the poster, and then we can add all the pictures in class on Monday. That should work, and that way we can make sure we all agree that everything's good before we turn it in. Just make sure it's neat when you do it."

The girls got up to leave, but the star-stealer wasn't satisfied. "I still don't trust him. Remember all those tests he failed? They weren't even hard! We did great on them and barely had to study."

"I'll do a good job."

The girls were clearly uncomfortable and just

wanted to leave. I think they felt bad for me.

"I've done great since then," I said. "I've been working really hard."

"I have seen him working hard," Jenna said. "I trust you, Max."

"So do I," Brianna agreed. "Besides, all he's really doing is copying the information we've already written down. And we can look over it Monday to make sure it's alright. Just make sure it's neat," she said again.

The star-stealer scowled at me. "Well I don't. Why don't you come over here tomorrow and we can do it together. My parents won't mind. The girls don't need to be here."

The girls edged their way to the door, "Sure, but we need to go. Get it done together or whatever. Just make sure it's done for Monday."

"Fine," I said.

I knew it was a bad idea. I'd do better by myself, but I couldn't put up a fight. I'd just be the bad guy all over again. I tried to be respectful.

"I'll come over here the same time tomorrow,

and I'll be sure to have the poster board."

The star-stealer snatched up the papers. "I'll hold onto these."

He practically pushed me out of the front door. My mom wasn't supposed to pick me up for another thirty minutes, but I was more than happy to wait on the front steps rather than inside with him.

And I knew tomorrow wasn't going to be as simple as copying information onto a poster.

Respect

It's an interesting word.

Everybody knows it, but I'm convinced that
most people don't really know what it means.

I mean, they know what it "means,"
but they don't know what it MEANS.

So here's your test (haHA!),
what does respect MEAN???

Help

The next day I made sure to take every supply I could think of. I didn't want to depend on the star-stealer for anything. I knew he was up to something. He wasn't exactly the hardest worker in the class, so I was suspicious he wanted to help out.

I had my mom drop me off at exactly the same time, went up to the front door, and rang the doorbell. He answered right away and was nice when he let me in, but right as my mom pulled away I knew something was wrong.

"There's been a change of plans."

His parents walked into the room and looked at me with a really confused expression.

"Hi," his dad said, though it sounded more like a question. "Are you coming with us?" He turned to his wife. "Did you know anything about this? Nobody told me. You never tell me all the details."

"No," she said, trying not to argue in front of me. "I don't know anything about this."

"He's just dropping off some supplies for the project," the star-stealer  said. "Remember that big one I told you about?"

His parents nodded.

Before I knew what was going on, the star-stealer practically tore my backpack off my shoulders and was rummaging through everything I'd brought. He took the poster board and a bunch  of the supplies. When he was finished ransacking my stuff, he tossed the backpack into my face. Then I guess he decided he didn't need some of the stuff he'd taken because I felt him stuffing things into my pockets as I wrestled with the backpack he'd thrown at me.

"There. That ought to do it. There was a change of plans and we're heading out. I'll get the poster done tonight. I already let the girls know."

"What's he talking about," I heard his dad mutter. "We've had this planned since Thursday."

The star-stealer ushered me out the front door along with his parents. They headed to the car, leaving me in their front yard still wondering what was going on.

"Do you have a ride home?" his mom asked, hesitant to get in the car and leave me stranded.

"I'm fine," I said. "I'll call my mom. We don't live that far away."

They were gone a minute later.

I sat down on the sidewalk, called my mom, and waited.

What was I supposed to do? Was the star-stealer actually going to do the poster? Did he just want to take all the credit for it? Or worse, was he going to show up Monday without anything and blame me for not having it done when I'd promised I would do it?

My mom picked me up and drove me home. I didn't say a word the whole time, and I could tell she knew something was wrong.

Parents always know, even if we think they don't.

She stopped the car in the driveway, but before I could get out she asked, "You know you're not alone, right?"

"What do you mean, mom?"

"Well, lately you've been working so hard, like you're trying to conquer the world all by yourself."

"I have to catch my star."

"By yourself?"

"Well, it's MY star. Nobody else can catch it for me."

"True, nobody can catch your star for you, but they can help you."

I laughed. "Not a whole lot of people want to help the crazy kid who jams lunchmeat up people's noses."

"That was a while ago."

"Would you forget if it happened to you?"

"No," she admitted, "but you need to learn to trust people. You need to accept help just like you need to help others."

I was confused. Was she telling me to trust the star-stealer? I knew I couldn't. He'd already set me up to fail and seemed intent on keeping it up.

She reached over and put her hand on my shoulder. "Who can you trust to help you?"

I thought. "There's one kid at school - Carlos. We hang out at recess and talk about our stars. I know I can trust him. We help each other."

"Anybody else?"

I thought about everyone I knew. I'd had

more friends before the fight, but now a lot of them looked at me more like a bully now. I'm pretty sure the star-stealer had been busy spreading rumors about me.

I shrugged. "Pretty sad, huh? One person I can trust."

She shook her head. "Is that really what you think?"

I nodded.

She squeezed my shoulder. "Honey, do you not think your father and I are here for you?"

"Well, yeah, but you're my parents."

"Yes, we are, and when you want our help, all you have to do is ask."

I looked at my feet. Why is it you always look at your feet when you're sad and thinking? When you're trying to remember you sort of look up, but when you're sad and thinking, it's always down.

Anyway, I thought about what my mom was saying and finally I said, "Mom, I do need your help, and I need it now."

I felt bad asking her to go to the store again, but I needed more supplies. She didn't fuss or ask questions or say a word. We just went to the store, got more stuff, and headed back home.

When we walked in, I went to my dad and asked for his help too. I could tell he and my mom were giving each other those secret parent looks, and he nodded that of course he would help.

The star-stealer had all the information, so I was going to need help looking it up on the computer all over again. If my dad hadn't helped, it would have taken me all night, and it nearly did anyway. I stayed up way later than usual for a Sunday night, but I had to. I had to be there for my group. I knew some of the information was different, and probably not as well-written as the girls had done it, but I finished it the best I could remember from when we'd talked about it in school the week before. And I did my best to be neat.

I went to bed thankful that I had help and wondering how tomorrow would go.

Gone

I woke up early Monday morning with a smile on my face. I got ready to go to school, and then my life fell apart.

Not piece-by-piece.

All at once.

Like an atomic bomb.

BOOM!

"Mom!" I screamed. "Mom! Mom, where is it?"

My mom rushed into my room half-asleep. "What on earth? What's wrong?"

"I can't find it! It's gone!"

"What's gone?" she asked. "Your poster is right there where you left it. Look. It's on the desk with your other school stuff."

"Not the poster," I said. Panicked, I tore through my dresser, pulling out all the clothes from every drawer and flinging them onto the floor.

"Stop," my mom said. "Max, you're making a mess!"

Not listening, I dove into the closet, then searched under the bed, and finally cleared everything off my desk with one huge swipe of my arm, sending everything crashing to the floor, including the poster I'd worked so hard on. The whole time my mom fussed and begged me to stop, but I didn't. I couldn't.

And then I slumped to the floor, lifeless.

"It's gone."

By now my dad and little sister were standing in the doorway gawking at the chaos.

"WHAT IS GOING ON?" my dad asked, not happy with what he was seeing.

"It . . . it's gone," I stammered. "My star. My star is gone. My star."

My sister snorted. "It's not gone, silly. Just think of the last place you remember having it."

And then it hit me.

I wouldn't misplace it.

I never would have lost it.

It had to have been taken.

But I always kept it in my pocket with me.

Wouldn't I notice somebody going through my pockets?

Unless I was too distracted to notice.

And I'd been too busy working on the poster all night to notice.

Of course it was him.

It had to have been the star-stealer.

When he was
stuffing things into
my pockets. He was
really just trying to
get my star.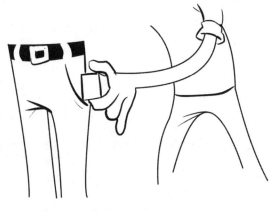

And he did.

My star.

Gone.

Speed Bump

I bet you can guess how I felt. Let's just say there was only one thing on my mind - the absolute decimation of the star-stealer.

I wanted to get to school as fast as possible, but instead I was almost late, again, because my parents made me straighten up my room before they let me even think about leaving. I quickly stuffed all the clothes I'd thrown around the room into the drawers, shoved things back into the closet, and piled a bunch of junk on my desk, which my parents said was fine for now since everything was at least off the floor, but that I'd need to go back this afternoon and fold my clothes, put things away in my closet, and organize my desk. I didn't care, just so I could get to school.

I nearly forgot the poster, but my parents had invested as much time and energy as I had and weren't about to let me leave it at the house.

When we finally got to school I tried to leap

out of the car, but instead my dad locked the door before I could open it.

"Now, I know you're upset. Have you thought things through?"

I tried to force the door open, but my dad wasn't having any of it.

"Have you?" he asked again.

"Of course," I barked. "All I've done is think about it."

"That's not what I mean," he said. "Think about ALL of it."

"Dad! I get it."

He frowned. "Do you? Because all those thoughts you've been having are about to lead to your actions."

"I know," I said, ready to pull my hair out. I tried the door again, but no dice. "I'm ready to put my thoughts into action, trust me."

"Son, look at me."

I rolled my eyes and looked at him for like half a second.

"Look at me," he repeated.

I groaned. "Fine. What?" I stared at him as hard as I could.

"Why did you work so hard on that poster?"

"For my group. I couldn't let them down."

He nodded. "Because you care about them. And you care about doing a good job. Right?"

"Yeah."

"Why?"

I didn't have any patience for this. "Because."

He waited.

"Dad, I'm going to be late for school."

He still waited.

"Because it's important. It matters. I'm trying to catch my star."

"Exactly. Think about that. Think about your star, and make it be a good thing that you're thinking about your star." He made sure I was listening and then continued. "Max, sometimes it's not the situation that's the most important thing, but your reaction to the situation."

I heard the door unlock, but now I didn't even feel like getting out.

I knew exactly what I was going to do,
until my dad talked to me.

Then I wasn't so sure.

What was right?

I thought about my star and
wondered what would help me catch it.

Have you ever been confused and torn
about facing a situation
because you weren't sure how to handle it?

Revenge

When I walked into the classroom I didn't even have time to unpack before the bell rang. I finished and hurried to my seat as quietly as I could so I didn't disrupt Mrs. Henderson starting the day. Then the star-stealer strolled into the room and walked right across the classroom like he owned it. He had a big smirk on his face, and then he turned, looked right at me, and winked. My blood boiled.

I imagined throwing my pencil at his head, but then I turned to the teacher and did everything I could to ignore the star-stealer, for now.

The day dragged on, but I was determined to focus on my work and listen to what the teacher said. It was hard. I was distracted, and I was still worked up from everything that had been going on. I thought weekends were supposed to be a break! I knew it wasn't my best morning ever, but I tried.

Finally the time came for us to get together with our groups and put any finishing touches on our projects before lunch and recess. I took a deep breath and went over to where the girls had claimed a spot in the corner.

"Where's the poster?" they asked. I could see the panic in their eyes.

The star-stealer strolled over. "Mr. Dependable here decided not to do any work. He barely stayed at my house for more than a minute before he bailed. Lucky for us I stayed up all night to work on it."

He pulled out the poster from behind his back and handed it to the girls, a smug expression on his face.

They looked it over and frowned. "Thanks, but it's . . ."

It was sloppy. It was messy. It looked awful, like he'd just scribbled things down as fast as he could to get it over with.

"It's not MY fault," the star-stealer interrupted. "I wasn't even supposed to be doing it. I just didn't want to let the group down."

The girls nodded. They weren't happy, but they weren't going to fuss at him when the blame was clearly on me. Jenna looked ready to cry while Brianna gave me a menacing look like she wanted my hair to burst into flames.

"Maybe we can ask for more time from the teacher to make it better," she said.

"Yeah. If we tell her about . . ." the star-stealer jerked his head in my direction. "It's not like it was OUR fault."

I just sat and waited, wondering how far he'd

go.

When they finished, I finally spoke up, "Actually none of that's true."

The star-stealer glared at me.

"I went over to his house," I explained, "and he shoved me out the door after stealing my supplies, among other things."

Our eyes locked. There was an unspoken understanding that I knew he had taken my star and that he knew I knew.

The girls shook their heads. "It doesn't matter what happened. This is what we have, and you didn't do any of the work, Max."

"I did," I said. "I did the poster."

The star-stealer laughed. "Are you really going to act like you did this?"

I got up and went over to my backpack. I pulled out my poster and came back.

"No. I'm not going to pretend like I had anything to do with THAT."

I laid my poster on top of his, and immediately the girls' eyes lit up.

"This is amazing!" they exclaimed together.

"Oh, thank you!" Brianna actually hugged me, which threw me for a loop.

The star-stealer bit his lip and narrowed his eyes. He glanced at the poster but didn't really look at it much.

"Yeah, thanks," he muttered. "You really came through for the group."

The girls went to work on the pictures and the finishing touches. They kept making comments about how good the poster was and how I'd saved them.

"And you didn't even have the notes, did you, Max?"

"Nope," I said.

The star-stealer sat back. He kept watching me. Then, as we were about finished, I noticed him patting his pocket. There was clearly a bulge, like he had a small box in it.

When he knew I saw it, he got up. He jerked his poster out from beneath mine and ripped it in half. He threw it in the trash and went back to his seat.

A few seconds later our teacher asked us all to get back to our desks. It was time for lunch, and then after recess we'd be presenting our projects.

Do-Over

I sat down at the cafeteria table, feeling pretty good about the poster. I didn't have much time to enjoy it, though, because the next thing I knew the star-stealer plopped down in the seat right next to me.

"Nice job with that poster, really." He opened his lunch and took out a sandwich. "I didn't think you had it in you. You really spent some time on that, huh?"

I nodded, even though it was obvious he wasn't complimenting me.

"I'll tell you what, if I'd known you were going to go through all that trouble I wouldn't have wasted the ten minutes I spent on mine. I figured next to you I would look pretty good."

"Why are you being like this?" I asked. "I'm sorry I shoved my sandwich in your face, but that was like a month ago."

He took his sandwich out and took off the top

piece of bread. It was a bologna sandwich. With mustard. A lot of mustard. Way more than any person would actually eat.

He laughed. The other kids noticed. Some of them smiled. Others turned away, not wanting to be part of anything about to go down.

I have to admit, that sandwich with all that mustard was pretty nasty, but I wasn't scared. Honestly, I probably deserved it.

"My dad helped me," I said. "With the poster, and with something else."

I reached into my pocket and pulled out a box just like I'd kept my star in. His face flashed a surprised expression, but he quickly covered it up.

"Nice box," he muttered. "Showing it off again, huh? You always have that stupid thing."

I pushed it toward him. "We both know this isn't my real box."

He smirked. "I don't know what you're talking about."

"Yeah you do," I said.

"Are trying to say something? Are you calling me a thief or what?"

I shook my head. "Look, I'm sorry. I know I apologized before, but we both know I didn't mean it."

He looked at me skeptically.

"But this time I do," I continued. "I had no right to do what I did. You spent your time making your box, and I smashed it without even thinking about what I was doing. And I smeared my sandwich in your face. I lost my temper, and I was a jerk." I could tell he hadn't seen this coming. "Nico, I'm sorry. I'm sorry for all of that. I've been trying to figure out how to chase my star, but I guess I'm just a pretty slow learner. I think I finally figured out that there's a right way and a wrong way to do things. What I did to you was wrong. If I want to catch my star, I can't be fighting people. I want people on my team."

I put the box in his hand.

"I know it's not as good as the one you made because you made that one with your own hard work, but I want you to have this one anyway. And my other one . . . well I guess I lost that one. If you find it you can have it, too. I owe it to you."

Nico held the box in his hands and stared at it for a minute. "But, that's your star, man. In that other box I mean."

"I know. And you can smash mine like I smashed yours, if that's what you want to do with it. That's what I deserve. That's how I treated you. And you can smash your disgusting sandwich in my face and all in my hair and whatever."

He shook his head. "I don't get it. Why are you doing this?"

"I'm tired of being the bad guy. I don't want to be a bully. They don't catch stars. I'm done with having 'episodes' and slacking off and just getting by. I want to be excellent. That's the only way I'll catch my star. I'm going to be greater than anything that gets in my way."

"But your star is gone. You can't catch it anyway."

I shrugged. "I guess not. Who knows, maybe I'll find another one." I looked at him. "Or I can help somebody else chase theirs. I've had help chasing mine. I guess I didn't get very close, but at least I got closer than when I started."

Nico didn't say anything else. He put his sandwich back in his bag and left to eat his lunch at the other end of the table. I glanced at him a few times, but I never saw him eat anything. He had the box I'd given him on the table in front of him, and he just kept looking at it.

He seemed sad, and I felt bad for him. I wondered if that's how my parents felt when they saw me struggling. I wanted to help, but I didn't know how.

At least I didn't get meat juice and mustard slathered in my face.

Unfair

After lunch we had recess, and I did what I usually did. I sat on the bench next to my fellow star-catcher, Carlos, only now I couldn't take out my star. It's funny because I still felt the same. I didn't feel empty or anything. It honestly still felt like I had my star. I knew what to think about. I didn't really need my box to know.

Then, about halfway through recess, something unusual happened, which was normal for the day since the whole day from the time I'd woken up was pretty strange.

Nico came and sat with us. He still had the box I'd given him in his hand.

"Hey," I said. "You alright?"

"Yeah." He sat there for a minute and nobody said anything, but then he said, "So, you guys sit here everyday and do the same thing."

"Yep," Carlos said. "It helps to have someone you can depend on."

"What do you guys talk about?"

"Our stars," I said.

"But aren't they different?"

"Yeah." I laughed. "They're actually completely different, but that doesn't matter. We can still help each other."

Carlos looked at Nico. "You know, you can join us anytime you want."

"Three's better than two," I agreed. "As long as we're all helping each other."

"Thanks, guys, but you don't want me here."

We started to disagree with him, but he waved his hand.

"Look, the reason I came over here is because I need to tell you something." He stared at the ground. I knew it couldn't be good. "I know you already know, but I did take your star. I'm sure you already figured it out. It was when you came over to my house and I was shoving stuff into your pockets."

"I know," I said. "But that's okay. We all make mistakes. I've done more wrong things than I can count. We can't let that stop us, though. Don't let it keep you down. It's just something to overcome. We're better than that."

"That's not all," he said, and he really dropped his head. "After I got home I went up to my room and . . . I didn't mean to, but I tried . . . I just wanted to know what was in your box. Mine never had anything in it, but I thought yours did because it meant so much to you. I didn't know if it was a star or what, but I figured there had to be SOMETHING and I wanted to know what it was.

So I tried to open it." He sighed. "But it wouldn't open. So I got a screwdriver and tried to pry the top off carefully. But it was stuck, and I had to really force it. When I did, the screwdriver ripped the top off and my hand slipped and I accidentally smashed one of the sides in."

I can't say I wasn't disappointed.

"Hey, so you broke the side. It's not that big

of a deal. I can fix it."

"That's not the really bad part," he said.

"What do you mean?"

Nico cleared his throat. "When the side broke
. . . I panicked."

I didn't want to ask, but I had to, "And?"

He looked at me, and I could tell he felt
worse than I ever had. "And I dropped it. I don't
even know what happened. I've thought about it a
million times. I don't know how, but when it hit the
ground it's like it was made of glass. It shattered
all over the floor. I swept it up to put back
together, but there was no way. I dumped it in the
trash because I didn't know what else to do."

"My star?"

"I'm sorry," he said. "It's gone. By now the garbage truck's taken it. It comes on Mondays."

I was speechless. I had convinced myself I would get it back. I'd overcome so much. I'd taken so many steps. I listened to my teacher everyday. I did my work, and I did it with excellence. I was respectful. I was polite. I helped out. Not because I had to, but because it was the right thing. I'd even turned my enemy into my friend. I had come so far, taken so many steps, tried so hard to catch my star. Now, though . . . I felt the life slowly drain out of me.

Somehow recess was already over.

I went back to the classroom.

My group presented.

I don't remember saying a word, but everyone said that we did great, that we nailed it, that we would probably get the best grade in the class.

I felt empty.

I didn't want to do anything.

The bell rang, and I went home.

I sat on the couch and turned on the television. I didn't even watch whatever was on. I just sort of stared in its direction.

How could my star be gone?

Why were things like this?

It wasn't fair.

I closed my eyes.

I didn't sleep. I just didn't want to open them.

Next

When I opened my eyes, my sister was sitting on the floor staring at me.

"What's wrong?" she asked seriously.

We usually don't talk that much, other than yelling at each other about all the usual brother-sister stuff. I'm used to her being too little to say anything coherent, even though now she's been in school for a couple of years and can talk just fine.

"Nothing," I said.

"Did you find your box?"

"Sort of."

"Then why aren't you happy?"

"Because my star is gone."

"I doubt it," she laughed. "You can't lose something you never had."

I sat up and actually looked at her when she said that. "What?"

"You didn't catch your star, did you?"

"No."

She shrugged. "So you never had it, and if you never had it, you couldn't lose it. It's still wherever it was."

I must have given her a funny look, because all of the sudden she stuck her tongue out and pranced away like she was a horse.

After she left, I couldn't get her words out of my head.

What if she was right?

I knew I hadn't caught my star.

Didn't that mean it couldn't have been in the box?

So what if the box was gone?

That didn't have to mean my star was gone.

Stars can't be that easy to get rid of.

But what was actually inside the box?

I'd never asked Nico if anything was in there.

I knew there had been SOMETHING inside.

I didn't know, and I think I was more confused than ever, but I felt a spark of hope come back to life inside me.

At dinner, I told my family all about my day. I usually didn't explain a whole lot, but as much as they'd done for me lately, I knew they deserved all the details.

They couldn't tell me enough how proud they were of me.

"See, isn't that better than ending up in the principal's office?" my dad said as he chuckled.

My sister laughed too. "Boys are so weird. Who would even put mustard on a sandwich to begin with?"

"Well you worked hard on that poster," my mom said, ignoring my sister's comment. "You did great, and you deserve it, honey."

"Thanks. Thanks for helping out. Everyone. I just wish I still had my box."

My dad gave me an odd look. "What's the box all about anyway that it's so important?"

"It's my star, or at least I thought it was. Now I don't even know."

He tapped his chest. "I don't know about a box. If you ask me, anything as important as a star should be kept in here. Nobody can steal that."

My mom nodded. "Do you really believe your star is gone?"

"I dunno."

"You said your star is what you think about, right? Well, do you still think about it?"

"Yeah, all the time."

"Then it's not gone. It can't be. Maybe you just have to find it again."

I snorted. "There's kind of a lot of places to look, Mom. It could take the rest of my life."

"I don't know," my dad said. He leaned back in his chair and winked. "Seems like that star has as much to do with you as you do with it. I wouldn't think you could be separated all that easily."

"Then you tell me where it is," I said, rolling

my eyes. Like it was going to be THAT easy.

My sister tugged on my arm. "You're not very smart sometimes. Why don't you look where it always is."

"It's not in my pocket," I replied.

"Stars don't live in pockets," she said. "Where did you find it?"

My eyes widened. I jumped out of my seat and was about to dart out of the room when I caught myself. My mom had worked hard on dinner, and I couldn't just leave.

She grinned. "Go ahead."

I didn't need to be told twice. I was out of my seat in a flash and skidding into my room before my dad finished laughing.

And there it was.

By the window.

On my desk.

Right where I'd found it.

Right where I put it every night when I went to bed.

My star.

Stars

Don't get me wrong. My box was a mess. It was cracked, bent, dented, scratched, splintered, and altogether not much more than a pile of scraps that were somehow barely held together. But it was my box.

And inside was my star. At least that's what I'd always thought. There was definitely something inside, something that gave off a bright golden light that burst through every crack.

I sat at my desk and stared at it for a while. I didn't dare touch it. I didn't want whatever was inside to spill out and disappear.

After a while though, I knew I had to try messing with it. I am a boy! Finally I picked up my box, but not a single chip came off the outside, and not a drop of anything leaked out from the inside.

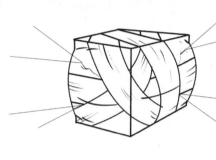

Even though the box seemed like it would somehow be sturdy enough, like some invisible glue was binding it together, I still felt like I had to do something. All I could think of was to pull out a roll of duct-tape and wrap it around a couple of times. It didn't look all that great, but I didn't care. I had my box. My star.

I slept with it beside me, and man did I sleep good. It was a peaceful rest.

At school the next day, my box was back in my pocket. As badly as I wanted to, I didn't take it out all morning. I paid attention and worked hard in class and waited for recess.

Finally it came, and I went to the bench, where two people joined me.

I took out my box, and the three of us examined it together.

Nico shook his head. "But how did it even get back to you? And all in one piece too. I'm not even lying when I say it was in a million pieces at the bottom of our trash bin."

"I don't know," I said. "At first I thought my parents tracked it down or something, but they said they didn't. Plus, they couldn't have known where it was."

Carlos cleared his throat. "I've been thinking about this a lot, ever since you said you were going to get rid of yours, Max. Remember when you were about to throw it away."

I nodded, ashamed I'd ever thought of doing such a thing.

"Well, I don't think you CAN get rid of it," he threw out. "Think about it - it's YOUR STAR. You can't just get rid of a STAR. I guess maybe it could fade away if you forgot about it or ignored it, but that's just because you're not looking for it anymore. As long as you're chasing your star, you'll always know where it is."

We sat there and grinned at each other for a minute. We probably looked pretty silly, all three of us on the bench sitting there just smiling.

Now, there's something I didn't tell you yet. I did it on purpose. I had to wait until the right time.

"Whoa!" Nico said when I let him hold it. "I can't believe it. It's at least twice as heavy as when I had it."

"I know." I nodded happily.

"And what's all that light inside? Is it really a star?"

Carlos and I glanced at each other.

"You mean you never saw it before?" I asked.

Nico shook his head. "It wasn't there before."

Carlos shrugged.

We had always seen it. We didn't ever have any good idea about what it was. That's why we always called it a star, but we had always seen it.

And it was definitely way brighter now.

WAY brighter.

But now, thinking back, maybe no one else had seen it all along.

Maybe that's why Mrs. Henderson hadn't seen any difference between my box and Nico's.

And maybe that's why kids didn't care much after the first day.

Except Carlos. He'd known it was real. He'd seen it, and it had inspired him to find his own star. And now Nico saw it.

"So, what is it?" he asked.

"I've been thinking about that," Carlos said, analyzing his box. He had the same golden light in his, and I saw it, and so did Nico. "I think it is a star."

"It can't be. That doesn't make sense," I said. "We haven't caught our stars yet."

"But we're chasing them. We're closer, and I think we might have even caught PART of them," he insisted. "Think about everything we've accomplished. I know it's not close to what we'll have to do to catch the actual stars, but we've taken a lot of steps. I think that when we make progress, we're actually capturing part of our stars. You know, like stardust or something. We're on the path to our stars, and along that path are little pieces of our star that we're continually collecting."

"That's why mine is heavier and brighter?"

"I think so. And maybe you never saw it before," he said to Nico, "because you didn't share in the dream. You didn't get it. You didn't care about it."

"But you do now," I added quickly. I didn't want Nico to feel bad. "You're part of our team now, so you're sharing our stars with us. They're not yours, but you can see them and you're helping us chase after them."

He smiled.

Carlos clapped his hands together. "Which

definitely means nobody can steal our stars. They're ours, and only people who share our dreams can even see that they're a real thing to us."

I nodded. "That's like my dad said. He said we should keep something as important as a star in here," I thumped my chest just like he did the night before, "because then nobody can ever steal it."

"I think it's like that a whole lot," Carlos agreed. "Our stars are safe with us."

I looked at my beaten up box. "But they won't come to us. It's not that easy. We still have to catch them."

"How?" Nico wondered.

"Well, what we've figured out is that if we do the right things and stay focused, we'll get there. It puts us in the right position and on the right path. It's slow, but it gets us going in the right direction."

Carlos smirked. "And as long as we're in the right position, on the right path, and taking steps, we'll be chasing our stars."

"And gathering more stardust," Nico added.

"Imagine how big of a box we're going to need!"

"I'm just worried about this one," I said. "I need a bigger box quick!"

Nico laughed.

Carlos stood up, excited. "It all makes sense now. Because you're closer to your star, you can see it more. It's brighter and heavier because you have more of it. And it's clearer because you know where it is."

"It definitely is. It's taken a while, but I think I'm starting to understand how it works.

When I started out, my star was just something I really liked. It was a passion. Now, though, I think I know what to do with it."

Nico looked at me. "Do you think there's a star for me?"

"No," I said. I waited a few seconds, and then just so he knew I was joking, I added, "I KNOW there is!"

How to Catch a Star

Carlos and Nico and I sat together at recess everyday for the rest of the school year. We helped each other. We overcame more struggles, because there are always more obstacles. We overcame more failures, because everybody makes mistakes. And before the year was over, Nico found his star. He even made another box, and it didn't look anything like mine!

As for me, I made a new box too. A bigger one.

Don't worry, I didn't get rid of my first box. It's way too valuable, which seems odd to say about something that's been destroyed and barely looks like it's holding together. But that's my box. And every scratch on it, every crack and dent and mark, is a reminder of how far I've come and how many obstacles I've gotten over.

On my worst days, I take that box out and look at it. And I know I can get past anything in my way. And I know that I'll catch my star someday. And I smile. And I laugh. I think of cat posters. I think of bologna and mustard. I think of how to turn anger and hate upside down to make a friend. I think of teammates who will do anything to help. I think of a little sister who's probably smarter than me. And most of all, I think of my star.

Because it's my star.

And I **WILL** catch it.

Just like you.

And your star.

Because we're dream chasers, star catchers.

We have grit.

We do the right thing.

We respect others.

We're overcomers.

We're greater than obstacles.

Greater than anything that keeps us from our stars, our dreams.

Greater than anything you can fill in the blank with.

Greater than . . .

Because we're star catchers.

Dream chasers.

So find your star.

Get your team.

And go.

. . . GO!

Now you know my story.

But that doesn't mean we're done.

As you know,
I still haven't caught my star.

And now there's you . . .

Look back at page 43.

If you want to chase a star, you have to figure out how to turn a passion into a star. That's something I can't tell you exactly how to do, but look at the list you made and ask yourself these questions:

1) Does it make you smile?

2) Do you enjoy learning about it?

3) Is it something you'll work for?

4) Is it something you'll want to do even when you're old?

5) Is it something that will impact people in a positive way?

If you're going to chase a star
this is something you HAVE to do:

Get a TEAM!

It took me a while to figure out
who was on my team,
but hopefully I can give you a head start.

First . . .

. . . list everybody who influences
your life on a regular basis.

Who do you listen to everyday?

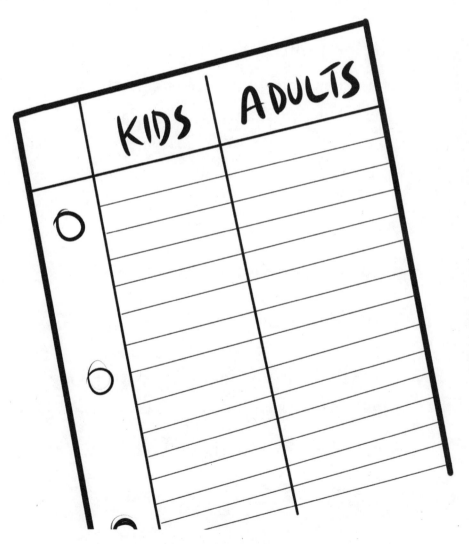

Now look back at your list and answer these questions about each person:

1) Can you trust them? Do you know they'll be honest with you (even if it's to tell you something you don't want to hear but that will make you better) and be there for you when you need them (especially if things aren't going good)?

2) Do they support you? Do they encourage you and let you know that you're doing a good job? Do they insist that you do a good job?

3) Do they help you come up with ideas? Will they listen to you and give you good feedback? Do they push you to be better and think more?

If there are people on your list who do these things (so you're saying YEP to a lot of my questions), then you want them on your team. Circle their names!

Okay, so here are some things that DON'T matter:

1) Are they "popular" or "cool" or whatever? That stuff's not really important.

2) Are they are a girl or a boy? Think about it - anyone can help you.

3) Are they your age? You read my story. Even I have to admit that some of the smartest stuff came out of my LITTLE sister's mouth. You can have people on your team younger than you. AND you definitely want an adult on your team. They're a big help!

Hopefully you've got an idea of who can be on your team, but this is important, so I want to be clear:

- Have an adult on your team. It can be a parent, but it doesn't have to be. It could be a teacher or a coach or an uncle or whoever, but have an adult who you say YEP to for most of those questions.

- Have the right amount of people on your team. Usually you only want a few people on your team. If you have like 20 people, that's crazy. You can't listen to that many people. I only had a few people on my team, so don't feel bad if you don't think you have that many names that you can circle. You should only have a few people who are THAT close to you.

Alright, I've only got one more BIG thing
for you to do right now.

Remember that word "grit?"

Well, YOU need it.

You've got to have the right attitude
if you're going to catch a star.

Check out the next page.

Grit is being determined
to overcome any obstacle.

When you're challenged, it's natural to want
to give up. You can't.

Something that helps me is to think about
obstacles I've overcome before.

It encourages me to know that
if I overcame THAT, I can overcome THIS.

Okay, so if you did all that stuff
I talked about on the last few pages . . .

- turning a passion into a star

- forming a team

- having grit

. . . then you are in position to chase a star!

You're on the right path,
facing the right direction,
and you are ready to GO.

And if you did all that . . .

. . . you're going to need this!

The Story Behind the Story

Every story has a story. *How to Catch a Star* didn't happen overnight, but instead came out of a program Stephen Vaughn developed called Xcel 2 Fitness. Through a void created from the loss of his father and a passion for wanting to make an impact on his community, Xcel 2 Fitness came to life. X2F's mission is to use the fundamentals of fitness to develop the character boys need to chase their dreams. The program was developed with the purpose of empowering boys to be fearless dream chasers and to give them the opportunity to reach for the stars. Not long after the start of Xcel 2 Fitness, Jason Pavelchak, a teacher, volunteered to coach X2F for his school. As Jason began to coach, he saw the effect it had on the boys and became more and more involved. Stephen and Jason started collaborating, and before long Jason began helping Stephen write the curriculum that is currently in place. As their passion to see X2F impact boys across the nation has grown, Stephen approached Jason about writing a book to depict a guide to chasing dreams. Just like the Xcel 2 Fitness program, the book's goal is to make an impact on the next generation and show that while it's not easy, everyone has a star they can catch. Stephen and Jason continue to work alongside each other both with Xcel 2 Fitness, as the program expands across the country, and with developing their next book(s). After all, you can't tell kids to be dream chasers unless you are one yourself.

Tell us about your dream. Email us at…

stephenrvaughn@gmail.com
jasonpavelchak@gmail.com

…and see how we're chasing our dream at xcel2fitness.com.